A Christmas Wish

and more stories of the season

Greg Borowski

Badger Books, LLC
Middleton, Wisconsin, USA

Copyright 2008 by Greg Borowski
All Rights Reserved
Published by Badger Books LLC
Illustrations by Jan Walczak
Printed in USA

ISBN: 9781932542387

Badger Books LLC
1600 N. High Point Rd.
Middleton, Wisconsin 53562, USA
Tel: 1-800-928-2372,
Email: books@badgerbooks.com
Website: www.badgerbooks.com

Also by Greg Borowski

First and Long

The Christmas Heart

To San On
Christmas wishes from
Memmer Catholic School

Greg Borowski

iv

For Katy,

who makes every day a gift

Contents

The Day Santa Was Late......................3

*"The man was heavy, but somehow light
on his feet. His face was wrinkled, but his
eyes danced even in the dim light."*

Sister Christmas..................................17

*"Then she sat by the window that night
staring into the stars, hoping – praying – to
see one moving as fast as a sleigh."*

A Christmas Wish.............................33

*"By now, his closet was full of boxes and
bags, but still nothing was quite right, no gift
was perfect."*

The Man in the Storm........................55

*" 'You can't change his moment,' the
man said. 'You can only change what happens in your moments, in your life.' "*

Snow Angel..79
"Bridget was still humming when she got off the elevator and saw the most surprising thing: A small box sitting on the floor outside her door."

The Boy Who Saved Christmas.........103
"So every year, as the wind blows colder, Santa Claus sets out into the world, always in disguise, on a quest to preserve Christmas."

Acknowledgments...............................123

A Christmas Wish

and more stories of the season

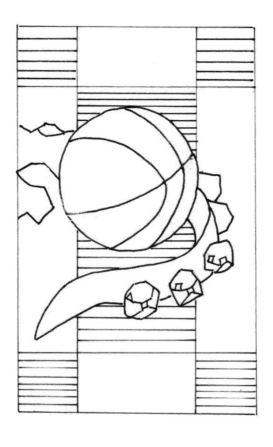

The Day Santa Was Late

The boots were always the hardest to get on, especially for Franklin Broyles whose back went out years ago. For starters, the boots were a size too small, and by the time Broyles had tied the pillow around his already-ample belly, he could barely lean far enough down to reach them.

When he did make it, he usually lacked the energy to tug the boots on, let alone stuff the red velvet pants inside. And, quite frankly, the boots were so tight they affected his circulation, causing him to spend long hours soaking in the tub at the end of each day.

That's not to say Broyles didn't like the idea of playing Santa at the department store, of sitting on the elaborate throne and watching the line of children who – it seemed to him – were a lot more impatient than when he was a boy. He remembered his own youthful visits well and he sometimes thought about them when there was a lull between the snap of photos. He remembered how slow the line seemed to move, how it inched through the men's department, through house wares, then hardware, then the toy department and – finally – the climb onto Santa's lap to spill out a year's worth of Christmas wishes.

No. Broyles liked the idea of playing Santa just fine.

It was just that he was new at the job – only his third week – and like the too-small boots, the job was not a perfect fit for him.

At 59, Broyles felt much more comfortable pushing paper and writing memos in his middle-management job at the bank, the job that provided him a tidy cubicle, a secretary he shared with another manager and, if he leaned carefully across his desk, a narrow view of the city's Christmas tree glittering with lights on the busy square below.

That is, the job that had been his until the day a pink slip arrived with his paycheck, stuck inside the envelope along with – Broyles was convinced the Human Resources Department never saw the irony – a card offering "warmest holiday wishes" and a gift certificate good for a frozen turkey or $25 in groceries.

So, that's what 37 years on the job bought these days: A sack of groceries.

And a feeling of shame so deep Broyles couldn't tell his family that to make a living he was now left to stuff a pillow down his pants, glue on a scratchy beard and spend four hours each afternoon wiping the drool of slobbering babies from his collar.

That was bad. But today would be worse.

Today was the day his grandson's scout troop made its annual trip to the mall to visit Santa. He had asked for the day off, even told his boss about Charlie and the whole situation. But the schedule stayed the same. Broyles could already picture Charlie, how he would be bursting with excitement as he neared the front of the line. How, after climbing carefully into his lap, there would be a moment of confusion, then of recognition, then a tremble of his lower lip and certain tears in the instant Charlie realized two things: There is no Santa Claus.

And his grandfather is a bum.

Broyles had tried to avoid the thought all day, but he could not. That morning he had trouble getting out of bed and only grunted when his wife, Miriam, asked over eggs and toast if anything was wrong.

How could he possibly say what was wrong? Not with his daughter there, and Charlie. The two had moved in a few months earlier, when times grew tight for them as well. Miriam said to look at it as a good thing, and by and large Broyles did. It meant more time with his only grandson, with whom he shared a birthday and a special bond.

It was a chance for them to read stories and play games and go on Saturday afternoon adventures. Meanwhile, Miriam was baking a whole lot more cookies these days and everyone, his daughter included, seemed happier than before.

So Broyles buried his secret.

"Everything's fine," he said, a delayed reaction to his wife's question.

Miriam looked over at him, sized up

the response.

"Good," she said finally. "Don't forget ..."

"My lunch," Broyles finished. "I know."

"And ..."

"Milk and eggs from the store."

He kissed her on the cheek and, wanting to avoid any shift in the conversation, picked up the sack lunch she had left on the counter. He mussed Charlie's hair – "Have a good day, champ" – and left, the door banging shut behind him. He pointed the car toward the office, but at the corner turned toward the library instead.

That had become his routine.

At the library he wandered among the tall shelves, paging through books of interest – Civil War, trains, sports. He read the newspaper front to back, filled out the crossword puzzle and took extra time reading the want ads, lost in the quiet until he realized he was 15 minutes late for the start of his Santa shift.

Now here he was, huffing after the jog from the car, hunched over in the tiny changing room – little more than a creaky bench, a locker and rusty sink – frantically pulling on the stupid boots. He grimaced with every echo of a child's voice through the air vents, echoes that only made the room seem smaller.

Finally, Broyles stood, adjusted his belt, scratched his chin and started fumbling through his bag for the sleigh bells, the ones he was instructed to shake and jingle as he walked down the hall so the kids knew he, Santa Claus, was on his way.

But he couldn't find the sleigh bells and he was already late, so without even a final glance in the mirror – his beard was slightly askew – Broyles grabbed for the door.

But it was locked.

Broyles tugged at it, imagining the worst. The door didn't open. He shook it. He rattled it. Nothing. He pounded on the door. No response. He shouted and pounded some more and saw the day crumble before him. The only thing worse than ruining his grandson's Santa visit was ruining the visit of all of Charlie's friends. He shouted again.

No response.

Broyles started to panic. Why weren't they looking for him? *They would have to come looking for him.* Had Santa ever been late before? *Not like this.* Could he be fired? *Yes.* Would he be fired? *Maybe.*

What then?

He could hear the muffled voices of the children, singing some Christmas carol along with the music that was piped through the speakers in the store's ceiling. Broyles leaned his back against the door, kicked at it a final time in frustration, then yanked off his beard – it stung more than usual – and collapsed onto the bench.

He sat for some time, running the past weeks through his mind.

He thought about the last day at the bank, how his career could be packed so neatly in one of those cardboard filing boxes. How even some of his longtime friends couldn't bear to make eye contact as he walked out, not wanting to admit if Broyles was downsized they could be, too. He had seen a few of his old co-workers at the mall, but always managed to turn the other way before they spotted him.

One day he had stopped to buy flowers for Miriam and a candy bar for Charlie, not thinking it would only provoke more uncomfortable questions. "Just because," he had said when asked. "No," he muttered. "Everything is fine."

Tired from the anger, Broyles finally dozed off, his head leaning against the cold wall. He didn't wake up for a few hours, until there was a noise in the hallway. He jumped to his feet and rushed to the mirror, figuring if he looked busy, somehow it might seem like just a mistake.

Broyles was adjusting the long white beard when he spotted a flash of red. He rubbed the mirror clean, looked closer and saw that it was a man in a Santa suit. A nice one at that. The outfit was a little newer, a little redder and much fuller than his own.

Broyles didn't know what to make of it all. His buddy Vince – laid off a month before he was – had the evening Santa shift. But this wasn't Vince. The man was heavy, but somehow light on his feet. His face was wrinkled, but his eyes danced even in the dim light. The beard was definitely real. As Broyles sized him up in the mirror, the two made eye contact. Broyles nodded and the man winked at him.

"Don't worry, they didn't miss you out there," the man said in a voice that was at once reassuring and a bit jolly. "And, if you're looking for a gift for Charlie, I'd recommend a new basketball this year."

"Charlie?" Broyles said, turning so fast he nearly lost his balance. "How do you know..."

But when he turned around, the room was empty. Broyles shook his head, blinked, and shook his head even harder. Yes. The room was empty. He was about ready to chalk it up to some crazy dream when there was the scratch of a key in the door.

It was his boss, Meredith, the too-serious manager of the toy department, her ever-present clipboard in hand.

"I wish they would leave this door unlocked," she said, propping it open. "Whenever I'm in here, I worry I'm going to be locked in."

"Well," Broyles said, irritated. "Now that you mention it."

Meredith continued talking, racing on as if she'd forget everything she had to say if she didn't blurt it out all at once. Broyles had learned to wait her out, so as she talked he glanced around the room, trying to figure out what had happened, since she didn't seem the least bit mad at him.

"You were great out there," she continued. "Just magnificent. I mean it always takes our Santas a few weeks to get the hang of it, but to fool your own grandson? Wow."

Finally Broyles spotted the answer to the mystery, right on the bench where he had fallen asleep – a set of silver sleigh bells, all on a worn leather strap, almost glowing from the shadows. They rested right where the man had been standing.

If there was a man.

"Now," Meredith said. "What's bothering you?"

"Nothing really," Broyles said, smiling now. "I was just wondering if you knew whether basketballs were still on sale? Someone told me Charlie might like one this year."

Meredith appeared confused, but Broyles did not notice. He sat down on the bench, kicked off the boots and picked up the sleigh bells, shaking them softly.

"No," he said. "Nothing wrong at all."

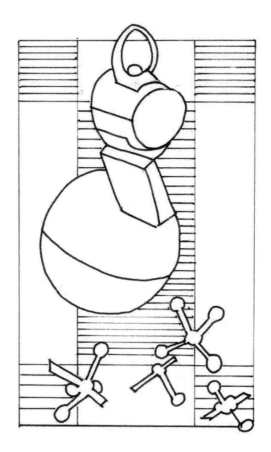

Sister Christmas

As the halls of Holy Cross Elementary School fell to quiet, the final bell having sent the students home to their Christmas break, Sister Mary Theresa erased the day's math lesson from the blackboard, brushed some chalk dust from her skirt and stopped to look over her classroom.

In the past weeks, the room had become the picture of Christmas. A construction-paper chain was strung from wall to wall and back again, the windows were a blizzard of cut-out snowflakes and the bulletin board sparkled with glitter-covered stars.

It was her first year at the school, and Sister Mary Theresa threw herself into the job and the lives of her sixth-grade students. The kids at Holy Cross, a small brick building tucked behind the church, were the children of the people who kept the city running – cab drivers and sanitation workers, waitresses and housekeepers, clerks and janitors.

Every morning, Sister Mary Theresa greeted her students in the doorway, offering a smile to each before she collected their homework. And at the end of the day, she gathered the students together and offered a blessing on them, a prayer of protection to cover the time until they were back in her care. It was just as the nuns, each in their heavy black habit, did when she was a girl. Playing that role now, she saw herself as less stern and not the least intimidating. How could she be at her size?

Now she turned to her final task before heading home – checking the room for lost mittens, stray pencils and anything else left behind. As she walked between the desks, straightening the chairs, she pictured each student.

There was Aaron and Evan and Will, Katerina and Alene, Erik and Ivan, Claudia and Callie, Megan, Joel, Hailey and even little Liliana.

But she couldn't stop thinking about the one who was absent: Gracie.

Gracie was such a sweetheart. She wore a fat pair of glasses, just like Sister Mary Theresa had at that age, glasses that hid deep brown eyes and sometimes got tangled in her hair. In class, Gracie was always first to raise her hand, always eager to run errands to the office or stay late to help clean up the classroom.

But Sister Mary Theresa knew Gracie had a hard time at home, where she and a younger brother lived with their mother, who tried to keep the family – and herself – together. There were days Gracie came to school without mittens or with her scarf untied. Sometimes she yawned through the first lesson, or took a nap at her desk during recess. But she never, ever missed school.

And now she was gone for the third time this week alone.

Sister Mary Theresa should have been happy that Christmas was here, eager to go to Midnight Mass with her nieces and nephews.

She went home worried instead.

The next night, Christmas Eve, Sister Mary Theresa called her brother and said she'd be late for the family gathering. She looked up Gracie's address, borrowed a car and set out to find her. She had to make sure she was safe.

Sister Mary Theresa knew where the house was, or thought she did, for she had moved to that very neighborhood when she was a girl.

She was 6 years old and her family had left a small apartment behind to start a new life in a new place. But then there came the night, just weeks later, when her aunt and uncle arrived, sent the babysitter home and explained there had been an accident and that Mom and Dad had gone to be with the angels. Her aunt and uncle stayed with them until they all moved away just after Christmas.

Sister Mary Theresa knew, somehow, it was all part of God's plan. She could see how it had steered her toward a life of compassion, toward working with children. But it had left a hole, a hole it seemed she could never fill. And she felt the hole was growing with each passing year, as more and more of those youthful memories slipped just out of her reach.

Now, driving down the narrow streets, a few of the memories fell into place.

She remembered that their house had wooden floors and dark closets and secret hiding places, spots where she could keep her toys so her brother couldn't find them. And she remembered how that Christmas, when they missed their parents so much, she and her brother scratched arrows into the floor so Santa would be sure to find the tree.

Then she sat by the window that night staring into the stars, hoping – praying – to see one moving as fast as a sleigh. She never did. But somehow, there were presents under the tree in the morning. She remembered her aunt explaining it as the magic of Christmas.

At that age, of course, the magic was in the getting.

Now Sister Mary Theresa always told her students that when gifts are exchanged, the magic flows both ways. There is magic to be found in the giving and the receiving.

As she drove, the sky grew dark and each street blended into the next, causing her to lose her bearings. There was a touch of snow in the air and it blew in the wind, obscuring addresses except on the few houses where Christmas lights blinked from the porch.

Finally, she found the house.

As she walked to the door, she saw an old plastic wreath hanging in the window. Suddenly, she wished she brought something with her, a toy or bag of cookies, a gift of some kind. But she had nothing to offer.

There were small footsteps, a curtain rustled and then a cautious but familiar voice from the other side of the door.

"Sister Christmas, is that you?"

That's what the students had started calling her, "Sister Christmas," since every day in December there was a new Christmas activity – an art project or a story or a song. The kids joked she should spell her name *Merry* Theresa.

"Yes, Gracie," she said, relieved to have found her. "It's me."

After a moment, the door opened. Gracie had an apologetic look on her face.

"Are you here for my homework?" she asked.

Sister Mary Theresa said she wasn't.

"I just wanted to check on you," she said with a gentle smile. "After all, you missed the blessing yesterday and it's a long time until school starts again."

She paused, sensing something was wrong.

"Is your mother here?"

"Oh, no," Gracie said, spilling out an explanation. "She just got a second job. Now she cleans at the hospital at night, so I have to do more around here. That's why I missed school yesterday, because Bobby was sick. I had to watch him. I just put him to bed."

Sister Mary Theresa couldn't leave yet. Not like this.

"I'm not supposed to answer the door," Gracie continued. "But I saw you coming through the window and I know it's cold out there."

Sister Mary Theresa stepped into the house, turning instinctively toward the living room, and quickly took stock of the situation. The TV was on, the picture fuzzy. In the dining room, a box of cereal and two empty bowls were on the table. And in the doorway, there was a box of Christmas decorations. A knotted string of lights sat on the floor, along with a wrinkled felt stocking. Gracie was trying to decorate.

After a moment, Sister Mary Theresa bent down and put her hand on Gracie's shoulder, whispering the familiar blessing that ended, "Lord, keep her always in your heart and in your arms." Then she pulled Gracie into a hug. As she did, she could feel Gracie tremble and sway. She looked into her sad face and a tear streaked down her cheek.

"Why, what's the matter?" she asked.

Gracie looked up.

"I don't think we're getting any presents this year," she said.

"But why would you say such a thing?"

Gracie said she had heard her mother talking, that money was tight. And after she put her brother to bed, she had searched all of the closets and the basement and didn't find anything.

"See, Bobby couldn't sleep," Gracie said, and started to cry again. "But I told him Santa was gonna come this year. I told him to just close his eyes and Santa would be here by morning."

Sister Mary Theresa had never felt so helpless. She wanted to promise there'd be a room full of presents in the morning, but she couldn't.

She didn't feel like Sister Christmas at all.

"Oh, Gracie," she said, trying to be of comfort. "That's more than a girl like you should have to worry about."

Gracie nodded.

She bent down and lifted Gracie's chin to look into her face. Gracie's eyes were still watery, and she sniffed back more tears. Sister Mary Theresa told her that they were a lot alike, in how they both were the oldest and how they both had to grow up so fast, too fast.

"You know," she said with a laugh, "one time I promised my brother that Santa Claus would find us. We even carved arrows into the floor so Santa could find the tree and have a place to put all the presents."

"Oh," Gracie said. "Our house already has those."

Sister Mary Theresa stopped and tried to read her face.

Gracie was serious.

"It does?"

"Right on the floor," she said, and pulled back the corner of the rug. "See?"

Sister Mary Theresa caught her breath.

She dropped to the floor and slowly ran her fingers along the faded lines.

This house, with its creaky floors and stained glass windows, it was her old house.

The two followed the arrows from the floor to the window seat, from the window seat to the doorway and then around the corner into the living room where, sure enough, there was a small tree in the corner, right where the arrows ended.

Seeing the tree brought back another memory.

"Gracie," she asked. "Is there still a closet in the back bedroom?"

"Yes."

Gracie's voice was full of confusion.

"You know," Sister Mary Theresa said, "Santa Claus will definitely be here tonight."

The two sat on the couch for a while and soon enough Gracie fell asleep. When she did, Sister Mary Theresa went to the back bedroom, turned on the closet light and bent down to slide her hand along the edge of the woodwork.

Finding the spot, she smiled and lifted up a floorboard.

She reached in and pulled out a small metal box and blew the dust off the lid. Inside, she knew, there would be everything she had hidden away so many years before: jacks and a rubber ball, a yo-yo, some toy cars and a whistle, a comic book, a bag of marbles.

She set the box carefully under the tree, a magic gift for Gracie.

And for Gracie's brother.

Then she sat in a rocking chair, and closed her eyes. When she did, she pictured a giant tree covered in lights and her brother, young again, a sparkle of mischief in his eye, and she could smell cookies in the oven and, she thought, she could hear the voices of her parents.

And that was gift enough for her.

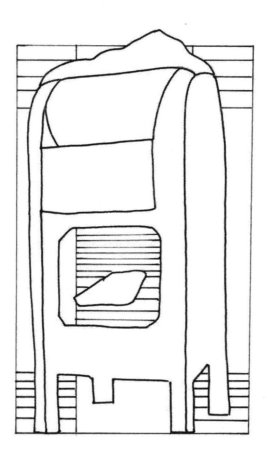

A Christmas Wish

It was an early December evening and the square was alive with Christmas. The trees were covered in white lights, the sidewalks busy with shoppers and the air filled with the youthful voices of carolers.

Maxwell Wagner stood in the middle of it all, a shopping bag heavy in each hand, chatting with yet another parent, wishing he could just slip away and get home. Dinner had to be made, though he figured Emma probably had spoiled her appetite with the cookies every store left out by the cash register.

Another parent walked up, more holiday wishes.

As the principal of Mapleton Elementary School, everyone knew Maxwell Wagner and everyone knew his sad story. His wife, Claire, had died a few months earlier, quite suddenly. They had a daughter, Emma, who had just started kindergarten.

And tonight, the annual "Christmas on the Square," would have been a night for all of them.

As the owner of a gift shop, Claire was the night's main organizer, cheerleader and spokeswoman. She placed the ads in the weekly newspaper, scheduled the music, even helped sponsor the town Christmas tree, now standing proudly at the square's edge, a star glowing at the top.

This year, she had led the drive to raise money for a new sculpture for the square – a life-size Santa Claus that would sit year-round on a park bench, perfect for photos, with its kid-sized lap. The statue was supposed to already be in place, but like so many other things, the fundraising had gotten off track.

Now, even the tree-lighting ceremony was running late.

Maxwell wanted to stay, but couldn't. With an apology, he started to leave.

"You hang in there," the mother said, gently squeezing his arm. "And be sure to give Emma a hug."

The words jarred him, as he realized Emma was no longer at his side.

Maxwell felt a twinge of panic.

He stepped away and scanned the crowd, his eyes darting from one group of shoppers to the next. He couldn't spot Emma and the panic grew. Was she lost? Missing? Hurt? Finally, he saw her across the street.

She was standing on her tip-toes at a mailbox, reaching up to drop a letter inside. But before he could register relief, Maxwell's heart sank instead.

It was her letter to Santa, he knew that much.

But Emma wasn't supposed to mail the letter, at least not yet, at least not until he had a chance to steam it open or hold it to the light, or to somehow figure out just what was on her wish list. He had to know so he could make this Christmas perfect and right.

In a moment, Emma turned and spotted him. She waved wildly and when the traffic cleared, she raced over, arms wide, mittens dangling from each sleeve. Maxwell set the bags down, dropped to a knee and caught her in a hug.

"I mailed it," Emma said proudly.

"Yes, I see that," he said.

"Do you think Santa will *really* get it?"

Emma's voice was hopeful and her eyes bright, two things that had gone missing in the past months. The same could be said of Maxwell, who sometimes wore a lost and befuddled look along with his wire-rimmed glasses. His face seemed longer and his hair a touch grayer. He even looked thinner, as if he wasn't eating right.

Claire's death had left him feeling as if he'd lost his footing. He hadn't quite fallen, but he couldn't seem to catch himself either.

Eager to leave, Maxwell checked his wrist and realized, once again, he had forgotten his watch.

"Why, certainly, Santa will get it," he said, reaching for the shopping bags. "You addressed it to the North Pole, right?"

"Yep," Emma replied, then added proudly: "I even drew a stamp on it."

With a few weeks to go until Christmas, the walls at Mapleton Elementary were starting to fill up with the traditional student artwork: construction paper trees, paper-plate Santas with cotton-ball beards, an entire herd of red-nosed reindeer.

A few days after the night on the square, Maxwell was looking over a new display when two boys raced around the corner. Spotting him, they slowed to a cautious walk.

"Sorry," one boy said.

The other boy was quick with an admonishment.

"Santa said we shouldn't run in the hallways," he told the first.

Maxwell shook his head and continued his walk. Each morning, he liked to walk the long hallways and listen to the echoes of the classrooms, lessons spilling from each open door, until they meshed together into one warm, comforting hum.

At the kindergarten classroom, Maxwell stood and watched silently from the doorway until – finally – Emma spotted him, lifting her head with a smile. Maxwell had found himself checking on her more frequently in recent days, as if to assure himself she was still there, safe in his building.

Maxwell offered a wave, then motioned the teacher, Mrs. Ryan, to the hallway.

He small-talked a bit, then got to the real question: Did she know what Emma asked for in her letter to Santa?

"No," the teacher said. "She said only two people could know what she wanted – I thought that included you."

"Emma told me the same thing," Maxwell said, with a frown. "But those people are Santa Claus and her mother."

After dinner that night, Maxwell brought up the letter to Santa again, but Emma wouldn't talk about it. He pushed a little bit, but Emma folded her arms. In the light from the lamp, he thought he could see a shake in her shoulders.

Maxwell was worried about her.

Sometimes when he came home from work, he'd find Emma sitting alone in Claire's closet – where the clothes still hung undisturbed – reading a book or playing with her dolls. One time he found her asleep, curled up on a pillow, one of Claire's jackets pulled down as a blanket.

Now, as they talked, Emma lowered her head.

"I wish Mommy was here," she said finally.

"We both do, honey," Maxwell said. "But, you know, you don't have to see Mommy to believe she is here."

They had gone over this before, many times, how sometimes you have to believe, no matter how hard it is. Sometimes you have to believe even when there is nothing to touch, no proof at all. At times, it was as if Maxwell said the words for himself as much as his daughter.

Emma nodded.

But after a moment, Maxwell made a connection, one that worried him even more.

"Did you ask Santa to bring your Mommy back?"

Emma shook her head.

"No," she said, then paused, as if about to correct herself. She tightened her mouth and then she simply shrugged. After a moment, she climbed onto Maxwell's lap, nuzzling her head under his chin.

He ran a hand through her hair, which was long and dark, just like her mother's.

Maxwell felt more unbalanced than ever.

At any school, the weeks before Christmas are among the most difficult of the year, attention spans as short as the light in each day. But this year something was different at Mapleton Elementary.

It was quiet.

The lines were orderly in the hallways. There were no fights at recess, no shouting in the cafeteria. In the morning, the boots were lined up in the cloakrooms. And at the end of each day, all the chairs were pushed in carefully behind the desks.

The students seemed to offer the same explanation, no matter what grade they were in:

"Santa said not to talk in the library."

"We have to put the toys away, because Santa is watching."

"Santa said our penmanship must be nice and neat."

Everyone had heard the comments, but no one thought much of them, least of all Maxwell Wagner who was worried more and more about finding the perfect gift for his daughter. Each day he bought something new, though sometimes he second guessed himself and went back the next day to return it. By now, his closet was full of boxes and bags, but still nothing was quite right, no gift was perfect.

One afternoon, as he walked past the square, a shopping bag in hand, he saw the most wonderful – and surprising – thing. The Santa statue. There it was, sitting on the park bench, gleaming in the fading sun. No one had even told him it was ready, though he was behind on his messages and may have missed it. Maxwell walked over to see the statue.

It was absolutely perfect.

Santa had a slight tilt to his head, as if he was listening to a child. There was a wink in his eye and a warm glow in his face. One arm was across the back of the bench, the other seemed to motion visitors to sit down. After so many months of plans and pictures, seeing the statue brought a smile to Maxwell's face, a comfort to his heart.

As he stood there, Maxwell remembered the times when he'd slip out of the building to meet Claire for lunch on the square. He could see her store, Simple Treasures, across the way. It was always filled with things you never knew you needed until you went inside – lockets and bracelets and sun catchers and note cards. He remembered how the bells always jangled when the door banged shut.

Now there was a sharp tug at his coat, yanking him back to the present.

"May I go now?"

The voice behind him was small.

"Huh?" Maxwell said, startled.

He turned and faced a girl he did not recognize. She was pointing at the statue. Behind her, a line had formed and Maxwell realized he was at the front. There were maybe a dozen kids, most from his school, all waiting quietly.

"Hi, Mr. Max," one said brightly.

He started to respond.

"May I go?" the girl asked again. She was very polite. She wore a long red ribbon in her hair and a fancy coat over a dark blue dress.

"Why ... sure," Maxwell said, taking it in slowly.

He stepped aside and watched the girl climb onto Santa's lap and begin talking, as if it was a real conversation, or at least half of one.

"Mr. Max, are you going to go?" a boy behind him asked.

"No," Maxwell said quietly. "No, it's OK."

"You can tell him anything," a girl said.

Maxwell looked at the statue for a moment longer, perplexed, and then returned to his walk home. When he got to the edge of the square, he looked back.

The line was longer still.

On the evening of the last day of class, four days before Christmas, the school held its annual Christmas pageant, an hour-long program filled with reindeer dances and snowmen songs.

As the crowd gathered, Maxwell stood outside the auditorium. He had already taken Emma to her classroom, where she joined an angel choir, complete with golden halos and aluminum-foil wings. As he waited, Maxwell spotted a familiar face – a young face – amid the parents, who swept through the doors.

It was the girl with the red ribbon in her hair, the girl from the park.

She walked directly up to him, offered a shy smile and, without a word, motioned Maxwell down. She stood on her toes and whispered in his ear.

"He said you don't believe."

A confused look crossed Maxwell's face.

"*What?*" he said, after a long pause.

The girl tried again.

"He said you say you believe, but really you don't."

She said it very simply.

"Who said that?" Maxwell asked.

They looked at each other for a moment, each unsure of what to make of the other. Finally the girl shrugged and lifted her hands. But before she walked away, she turned and said one last thing.

"He said you knew where to look."

With that, she disappeared into the crowd and before Maxwell could go after her, a teacher walked up. He was needed backstage. It was time to introduce the first act. Amid the rush of the evening, the strange encounter was quickly forgotten.

At the end of the night, Maxwell carried a sleeping Emma upstairs to her bedroom, taking off her wings before laying her down. He walked to his own room and sat down to take off his shoes. As he did, he noticed a sliver of light from beneath the door to Claire's closet.

"Oh, Em," he said, annoyed Emma had left the light on.

He went to the closet, but instead of turning the light off, he stepped inside.

It was all just as Claire had left it, blouses and dresses and jackets and skirts. He couldn't bear to give anything away. Maxwell looked over everything, running his hand along a hanger and then – *He said you knew where to look* – he remembered the top shelf, the one so high up that Emma couldn't even see it, the one where he knew Claire sometimes hid the presents.

Maxwell got a chair, stood on it and reached his hand around, sliding it back and forth, until finally it touched something – a small box, and then a second box, about the same size. He took them down and looked them over.

It can't be, Maxwell thought.

But he recognized the standard blue paper and gold ribbons of Claire's store. There was a note taped to each. One read, "Love, Mom," and the other said, "Love, Claire."

She always did plan ahead.

His heart ached at the thought.

On Christmas morning, after all of the other presents were opened, Maxwell took the boxes from behind the tree and handed one to Emma, saying something he thought he'd never say again: "This is from your Mom."

Emma's eyes grew bright, bright as the morning sun.

"I knew she'd remember," she said, her voice filled with certainty.

She carefully untied the bow and pulled back the paper, folding it into a small square before opening the box. When she took the cover off, it revealed a small gold locket shaped like a heart. And when she opened the heart, inside was a photo of Claire.

Emma hung it around her neck, opening it every few minutes to look at the photo.

In his box, Maxwell found an old-fashioned pocket watch, complete with a chain, so he wouldn't lose it. He had never been so happy and so sad at the same time.

After breakfast, the two drove to church, a light snow falling on the windshield, the flakes drifting and dancing in the breeze. As they passed the square, Maxwell slowed to point out the new Santa statue to Emma.

But it was gone.

There was no statue there at all.

His heart jumped. He pulled to the curb, yanked open Emma's door, took her hand and they rushed across the square. Emma strained to keep up, unsure what was happening. They got to the empty bench and stopped.

"It was here," Maxwell said.

He turned in a slow circle, and Emma did the same.

"What was here, Daddy?"

"The statue."

But a sign was tacked to the bench, just as before, noting the statue had been delayed. Emma started to read the words, carefully sounding them out.

"March," she said, when she reached the end.

"Yeah," Maxwell said, still scanning the square, his eyes settling on his wife's store. "Three more months, I guess."

In the distance, a church bell rang and Maxwell took out the watch to check the time. When he did, he turned it over in his hand and, in the glare of the sun, realized for the first time there was an inscription on the back.

Emma turned over her locket and found the same message.

It was a single, magic word: "Believe."

The Man in the Storm

The bus ground to a stop, sending a shudder through the passengers crowded in the aisle. The buses were about the only thing moving in the thick, gray morning, the downtown streets still smothered with snow.

The rain had changed to snow around midnight and the snow was still falling. It was wet and heavy, mixed with an unusual fog and even some thunder, a combination the forecasters said hadn't been seen for years.

John McNeal, talking into his cell phone, leaned across the woman next to him and rubbed the window clear. He never drove when there was a heavy snow. The bus was just as slow, but at least he could get some work done on the way to the office.

"I'm right outside," he said into the phone, then shouted: "My stop."

The passengers grumbled as he jostled to the front, offering random apologies as he rattled instructions into the phone, so intent on making the deal he never saw the burly man in the old plaid jacket pushing his way down the aisle, dragging a battered duffle bag behind him. The two collided, sending McNeal's phone skittering across the wet floor. He dropped to his knees, patting his hand under the seat where it fell.

He could feel the bus pulling away.

"Hold on," McNeal shouted.

"Next stop," the driver said over the din.

McNeal felt the phone, grabbed it and

stuffed it in his pocket as he stood up, angry. He was face to face with the old man, who began an immediate ramble.

"You look past it, right there in front of you, never stop and see," the man said. His face was wrinkled, his hair white, his beard full and his words a garble. "Must apologize, not me, you."

McNeal sized him up as a street person.

He could feel that people were already staring and certainly didn't want a scene. The bus slowed to a stop just in time, its door opening with a loud hiss.

"Sorry," McNeal said quietly, pushing past and out into the cold.

That afternoon the firm closed early, since it was Christmas Eve, sending everyone home for the holiday. McNeal was picked up by Allison, his girlfriend of two years. They went back to his apartment where they soon had the stereo going –

some pop singer doing Christmas stan-
dards – and a sheet of cookies warming in
the oven. The day had been filled with
meetings and, realizing he hadn't checked
messages, McNeal went to dig the cell
phone out of his coat pocket.

"Shoot," he said, frustrated.

Allison stepped into the living room,
drying her hands on a towel.

"What is it?" she asked.

"It's not my phone," he said.

"How can that be?"

McNeal retraced his day, settling on
the encounter with the strange man on
the bus. After he dropped his phone, he
must have picked up someone else's by
mistake. After some debate, they decided
to check the messages to see if they could
determine the owner.

McNeal pressed the voicemail button,
but instead of providing the messages the
sweet electronic voice asked for the pass-
word. McNeal started to ask Allison what

to do, but as he did, he noticed a key seemed to light up.

As he pressed it, another lit up, then another and another.

He shook his head, figuring it was just a reflection from the lights on the tree, but the voice soon answered back: "You have 317 new messages."

"Popular guy," he said, shrugging.

Allison gave a questioning look and McNeal waved it off.

"Just a lot of messages," he said.

The first message came:

"Santa, this is Billy. I've been really, really good this year. I'll leave the cookies out for you on the table. OK, bye."

Intrigued, McNeal saved the message and went on to the next.

This one was a girl.

"Hi Santa, this is Sara. I want a doll that has eyes that blink and a new outfit and ... and ... well, I guess that's it. My mom says to say thank you ... so, thank you."

The voices were small and nervous.
Some were barely clear over the static.
Madeline wanted a book. Julia wanted a
sled. Matthew a train, his brother a truck.
On and on the requests went. McNeal
soon gave up, but Allison kept listening,
offering a play-by-play of "isn't that dar-
ling" and "this is so sweet."

McNeal watched her face and could see
where the conversation was headed. Kids.
Commitment. The usual. Whenever they
had a disagreement, it always seemed to
circle back to the same thing – Allison
ready to grab life and move forward,
McNeal somehow paralyzed by the
thought.

Indeed, he had tried to move everything forward. On his rare lunch hours,
he would slip into the jewelry store near
his office and stare into the cases, sometimes letting a clerk show him a few rings,
the diamonds twinkling in the light. But

he always left empty-handed, only to return a few days later.

"Just let it be, Allie," McNeal said now, his voice low.

"Oh, this one is so cute," she said. "You have to listen."

As she held out the phone, it rang, startling them both. For a moment, they were unsure what to do.

The phone rang again. McNeal took it.

"It's just a phone call," he said, and pressed the button to answer.

"Hello," he said.

"Santa? This is Angela."

"No, this isn't Santa," he said sharply, then caught himself. "Angela, could you put your mother on?"

He heard a trembling sniffle, then an angry adult voice. McNeal talked to the woman for a minute or two, finally hung up and tossed the phone on the couch. He ran a hand through his hair, brown with the first flecks of gray. Then, without a word, he went to stand at the window.

The snow was still coming down, wet and heavy. It came with a strange fog that hugged the ground and there was still the occasional rumble of thunder in the distance. It was as if the weather was flirting right on the margin between rain and snow, the mere difference of a degree able to make it all of one or all the other.

Somehow the scene was both familiar and unsettling.

"Well?" Allison said finally.

"She said they called the Santa Line from Foster's Department Store," McNeal replied.

"Great," she replied. "You can call them and switch phones."

He turned, his face blank.

"Foster's went out of business years ago."

They talked about it as the cookies finished in the oven. Allison had grown up elsewhere, but McNeal knew all about the old Foster's Department store, which boasted a huge Toyland display, complete with a snow castle and elf village. It opened a few months before Christmas and featured a Santa Line that allowed children to call and leave their wishes for Santa. When they did, an elf would call their parents back, provide the rundown of wishes and – of course – offer to hold the items with just a credit card number.

McNeal heard all about Foster's every night over dinner.

His father operated a dime store, McNeal & Son, located a few miles away from Foster's and fretted constantly about the new store, with its wide aisles and its lunch counter and its huge, low-price selection. His own customers quickly dwindled, his profits along with them.

"He figured it would put him out of business," McNeal said. He rarely talked about his father, who had died long ago, except in bits and pieces, a series of dots never connected to form a full picture. It was a door McNeal wasn't ready to open, and he certainly hadn't told this story. "Of course, before that could happen ..."

"Wait," Allison said, interrupting. "I have the perfect idea."

"What?"

"The next kid who calls, we'll go get the gift and leave it on the porch or something." Her face lit up as she talked. "That would be so cool, don't you think?"

To be sure, the phone and the messages were all very strange. But the two had decided that whatever was happening, the calls were coming from real children, ones bound for disappointment in the morning. That much they had agreed on.

"Just the next one," she said.

Her hair was pulled back, the way she wore it when working in her studio. She kind of rocked on the balls of her feet.

Her eyes were bright, her smile ever hopeful.

Oh, how McNeal was a sucker for that look

But, try as he might, he couldn't adopt Allison's carefree approach to life. She was always happy and upbeat, the sort who would plug the parking meters of strangers. Sometimes, when her day was off to a bad start, Allison would purposely slow down to catch a stop light, figuring if she shifted her day by a single moment, everything would turn out differently in the end. To her, that shift could bring an unexpected hallway conversation or a surprise encounter with an old friend, could make the difference between buying a losing lottery ticket and the winning one. "Nothing is ever set," she would often say. "You can change everything, just like that, at any moment."

He did not believe that. No. For him, everything was fixed. Indeed, everything of today was locked into place on one night long ago, a night that had left him distant and detached, unable to commit to the future, to relationships, to most anything.

And McNeal could never change it, for he was the one who had caused it.

The phone rang again and, after a moment, it beeped to signal a message.

"OK, write this down," McNeal said, listening. "Jack ... age 7 ... he wants a race car ... OK, he's leaving a phone number."

"This is perfect," she said. "I'll grab my keys."

"No," he said, clicking off the phone. His face was drained of color. "I don't think we can do this."

"Why not?"

"The number ... I know the number." He was stammering now. "I mean, I mean, it's not my number from today."

"What are you saying?"

Finally, he steadied his voice.

"I think," he said, "that was me on the message."

McNeal finished the story now. When he was 7, he had waited until Christmas Eve to call the Santa Line, even though he knew he wasn't supposed to. He called after school, leaving the phone number of his father's store, to be sure his dad would get the call from the elf. But his father's store didn't carry his requested Streetrod Racer, so his father closed early to go to Foster's to buy it. McNeal had always pictured his father hunched over the steering wheel, muttering about having to make the extra stop, at Foster's of all places, when he should have been headed home instead.

"The roads were slick," McNeal said. "It was a strange storm, one that mixed thunder and rain. And there was, there was an accident and ..."

His voice had a small tremble.

"I never forgave myself," he continued.

"Never. I just had to ask for something more."

"Wait," she said, interrupting. "Thunder?"

"I'm trying to tell you how my father died," McNeal said calmly.

He stopped.

"Yes, thunder. It was a crazy storm, just like this one."

"And what time did you call?"

"I don't know," McNeal said, raising his hands in frustration. "It was after school, so maybe around 4 o'clock."

She looked at the clock above the fireplace. It was just before 4 p.m.

"You know ..." she began.

They debated what was happening. Was it really him on the phone? Impossible. But, McNeal acknowledged, it was too much for a mere coincidence.

If it was some sort of bizarre link to the past, what did it mean? Could he – even now, more than 25 years later – go back and stop his father? Could he go back and change everything?

No. That was crazy talk. There had to be something logical, something rational to explain it all. It had to be the weather, a faulty transmission tower. Something.

And yet ... and yet ...

"What do you think happens if we go there?" McNeal asked.

He searched her face. She looked at him, eyes intense.

"What happens," she said, "if we don't?"

As they drove past the bright store windows, Christmas lights glowing from behind the frost, McNeal realized he had not been down this street for many years. He had no desire to see what had become of it, to revive all the memories it held.

Now he was surprised at how familiar everything looked, as if he knew what would be on every sign, in every window.

Then he saw it and gasped.

"McNeal & Son."

The sign, with its bold blue letters, hung over the doorway. It was an ambitious name for the store, since the son – Jack – was just a boy when it opened.

Allison saw it too and pointed.

"That shouldn't be there," he said, mystified.

The store had gone out of business soon after his father died.

Indeed, everything from the past was back, the cigar store, the bank, the women's store, with its row of fur coats at attention in the window. Allison slowed the car, the slush splashing under the tires, and McNeal saw a movement near the door of his father's store.

A man was locking the door, his back hunched to the cold. McNeal's heart jumped. He stole a glance at Allison, fumbled with the door.

"Dad!" he shouted, climbing out.

The man turned. McNeal stumbled over a snow bank, stomped his feet on the clear sidewalk and squinted into the glare from the street light.

"Who is it you're looking for?" the man asked gently, stepping out of the shadows.

McNeal was confused. It wasn't his father. It was the old man from the bus that morning, the one with the crazy ramble.

"No one," McNeal said quickly and turned to go. "I'm terribly sorry."

"Are you sure, Jack?" the man asked, stepping closer.

In the light, McNeal saw that his face was cleaner than before. He no longer looked homeless at all. McNeal waved for Allison to start the car.

"Yes. Sorry."

But then McNeal stopped. He hadn't been called Jack in years.

"Who are you?" he asked.

"You're no longer that boy I remember," the man continued, as if McNeal hadn't even asked a question. "But every day you try to reach him. I know you do."

McNeal stood, his mind racing as fast as his heart.

"Your father is gone Jack, and of that I am sorry."

"I know," McNeal said. "He's dead."

The man continued, raising his voice slightly, as if to correct McNeal.

"He left no more than 10 minutes ago, determined to get a gift for you. It's too late to catch him. But that was his choice in his moment. You can't change his moment. You can only change what happens in your moments, in your own life. Weren't you listening to what I said this morning on the bus?"

The man repeated the words from the morning, which came clearer now. McNeal struggled to process it all.

"It's always been right in front of you, but you never stop to see," the man said.

"You must apologize to yourself Jack, not to me or anyone else."

The man paused, then continued, his next words offering a gentle nudge.

"If you give the guilt away, maybe you will receive something in return."

The wind blew, hard and cold.

"Getting colder," the man remarked, casually looking up at the sky.

The snow was starting to come heavier now, the sleet and rain fading into the cold. And McNeal felt the moment, this strange and amazing chance, was about to be lost, freezing everything as it had been before.

McNeal took the phone from his pocket and punched in a familiar number. Through the static a voice – his youthful voice – came on the line.

"Hello?"

McNeal wasn't sure what to say. He heard a rumble of thunder in the distance, then the echo of it through the phone.

"Jack?" he asked.

"Yes." The voice was excited. "Who is this? Is this Santa?"

McNeal paused, swallowed.

"Yes," he said quietly. "Yes, this is Santa."

"Mom! It's Santa!"

"Jack, listen," he said, reaching for the right words, words just beyond his grasp. "You know, sometimes you don't get what you want for Christmas. And ... and it doesn't mean you were bad –"

"Mom says I have to go. We're baking cookies."

The wind blew again.

"It's not your fault," McNeal blurted out. "Whatever happens tonight. You must always believe that. Promise me you will."

There was a pause, and McNeal hoped he had gotten through to Jack, gotten through to himself.

"OK, Santa. Goodnight."

There was a click and the static was replaced by the hum of a dial tone, then the honk of a car horn – Allison, suddenly impatient. McNeal looked up now. The man was gone. And all was different. The sidewalk was un-shoveled. There were no footprints on it at all, other than from his own climb over the snow bank.

The store was different, too. There was a security fence across the door, no toys in the window, just a neon sign blinking an ad for pay-day loans. The block had returned to its ramshackle look of today. McNeal shivered. It was colder.

He climbed in the car, the headlights cutting through the streaking snow.

"I really thought we would catch your Dad," she said. "Somehow, I just thought it would work."

"No," McNeal said, confidently. "It wasn't about him. It was about me."

He patted his pocket for emphasis, expecting to feel the shape of the phone but a confused look crept across his face. The phone was gone. Instead, he felt a small, square box. He had never seen it before, but somehow knew what he would find inside – a diamond ring blinking in the dim light.

And like the rain to the snow, the difference of a degree, he knew the phone call he had made – shifting his own life, just enough to ease the guilt – had changed everything.

He knew it because when Allison saw the ring and smiled and a tear came to the edge of her eye, his life, once so unsettled and uncertain, felt so right and warm.

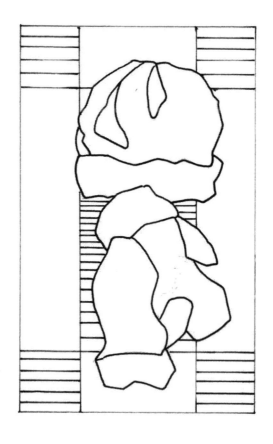

Snow Angel

On a cold, gray day in December, as the bus rumbled across the city, Bridget Monroe found herself looking out the window and dreaming of the warmth of home. For Bridget, a freshman at the local college, home was California, which – with Christmas approaching – seemed far, far away.

With every stop, another memory from home fell into focus.

She thought about how the house would be decorated, every corner of every room. About how the tree would scrape the ceiling, ornaments filling the branches and presents spilling out onto the carpet. About trays of cookies baking in the oven, the comforting smell filling the kitchen.

Bridget had tried not to think about home, tried to stay focused on her life here, but as each day arrived colder than the last, it was harder and harder to do.

She had stayed on campus because her parents were traveling overseas – a sudden business trip for her father – and wouldn't return until New Year's Day, when a delayed family Christmas was planned. Staying behind meant she could work some extra hours at the mall, getting a jump on tuition for the second semester, and she could finish her volunteer work at Fitzgerald Elementary School, part of her teaching major.

Her own semester had ended more than a week ago, leaving the campus – which was so lively when she arrived in

August – feeling emptier than ever. So the visits to Fitzgerald had become the lone bright spot in the month.

From stop to stop, her day-dreaming continued: shopping trips to the mall, caroling with the neighbors, stockings lining the fire place, lights tracing every window. Of course, the sun would be shining, the sky wide and blue.

And it would be so warm, so much warmer than here.

As the California scenes dissolved back into the cold Midwestern present, Bridget pulled her jacket tighter, leaned against the window and watched the city as it emerged from the morning darkness. The sidewalks were mostly empty, but a few stores were coming to life. The trees that lined the street had lost their leaves months ago, the twisted branches still waiting to catch the first snow of the season.

That triggered another memory: The last day of exams.

"It won't be so bad being here," Jen had said when she stopped in Bridget's dorm room to say good-bye. "Just think, you'll get to see your first snow."

"I know," Bridget replied. "I can't wait."

But her smile was a second slow in coming and it was thinner than usual, so Jen stopped at the doorway and tried again to cheer her up.

"I'll be down to pick you up on Christmas Eve," she said. "My parents already have the guest room waiting."

"I know, that's so great."

Jen lingered longer.

"Are you sure you're going to be OK?"

"I'll be fine," Bridget said. "Really."

But every time she walked past the darkened windows of the library or heard the echo of her own footsteps in the student union, she felt more and more alone. Now, with the last day of classes at Fitzgerald, her lone bright spot was about to go dark.

"No," Bridget said out loud, answering the conversation she had just replayed in her mind. "Not so fine."

As she said it, she realized the bus had stopped and several of the other passengers – all regulars on the route – were looking in her direction.

"Sorry," she said, standing up and rushing to the front door.

"You have a good day," the driver said. "And take care of those kids."

"I will," Bridget said.

Stepping outside, she pulled her hands inside her jacket sleeves, then stuffed her hands deep into her coat pockets. She kept forgetting to buy mittens and a hat at the mall. Shoulders hunched toward the wind, she walked the final two blocks.

In the distance, she saw the row of yellow school buses lining the curb. Behind the buses, cars and minivans were pulling up, as parents sent their kids off for the day, backpacks in tow. Bridget found herself walking faster until she stepped into the blur of activity on the playground – kids playing tag, bouncing balls, chasing from one fence to the other.

"Miss Monroe! Miss Monroe!"

She looked up to see Isaiah, a boy from her second-grade class, running up to her, arms wide open, expecting to race into a hug. Bridget bent down and caught him, his happiness lighting her own face. She closed her eyes for a moment and smiled.

"Guess what?" he asked

She took Isaiah's hand and they began walking to where his class was lining up.

"What?" Bridget replied.

"It's the last day of school," Isaiah said.

"I know," Bridget said. "Have you been counting the days?"

"Yep," he said, a special pride in his voice. "Just like you said I should."

Yes, for Bridget Monroe, the visits to Fitzgerald Elementary School were the bright spot of her long, gray December. During her own semester, she could only spend a few hours a week at Fitzgerald. Now she was spending the whole day, though she found the time passed just as quickly – math, science, vocabulary, recess, quiet time, lunch, then her one-on-one reading time with the kids.

For that, Bridget took her spot in the hallway, squeezing her knees beneath a small table, where she would greet each student with a smile. Some were ahead of the class and raced through the assignments, while others would take it syllable by syllable, slowly sounding out each word. She would gently correct their mistakes and, day by day, watch them improve.

The students always came in the same order: Marissa, with her long blonde hair; Mason, with his freckled face; Gabriella, with her perpetual giggles; then Isaiah with his bright, sly smile.

He had fast become Bridget's favorite.

Sometimes, of course, it was hard to keep Isaiah on track, as he spilled out his stories of super heroes and dinosaurs. He could be distracted by the posters on the walls, scuff marks on the floors or just a teacher walking down the hallway.

But he tried hard, so hard. When he stumbled on a word, he'd wait for Bridget to pronounce it, then would repeat it three times. After the third, he'd squeeze his head and admonish the word to "just stay in there."

Today, the two had somehow gotten onto the question of snow. Specifically, how Bridget had never seen snow before.

"So you never made a snowball?"

"Nope."

"A snowman."

"Never."

"Well, you must've made a snow angel?"

"A what?"

"A snow angel," Isaiah repeated, the words echoing the disbelief on his face.

Bridget was still confused.

So, Isaiah plopped himself onto the floor, stretched out his arms and legs and swept them along the tile, explaining the process. He slowly stood up, careful not to disturb the imaginary snow and the imaginary angel.

"See," he said. "When you get up, it looks like an angel."

"I can see that," Bridget said, nodding. "Very nice wings."

She checked her watch and realized their time was nearly up. So she coaxed Isaiah back to the table and she wrote out a list of things for him to work on over Christmas break.

"Read something every day, OK?" she asked.

"I will," he said, though his face turned suddenly sad. "But I always do better when you're here."

Bridget felt her heart sink. After all, she did better when she was at the school, too. She leaned forward in her chair, tucked her long hair behind her ears and put her elbows on the table. It was the technique discussed in her classes – put yourself on the level of the students – but for Bridget it was a natural thing.

"You know what?" she said, checking his eyes to be sure Isaiah was listening. "Whenever you think about a person, if you think really, really hard, it's just like they are actually there. Can you do that?"

Isaiah nodded.

Bridget took a small pin off her jacket, a ceramic angel, and pinned it to Isaiah's sweater and continued.

"But just in case," Bridget continued, "this is going to be your guardian angel."

A smile crept across Isaiah's face, but without a thank you – without any word at all – he turned and ran back to the classroom. Before Bridget could follow him, the next student – Lashaun, the quietest of the bunch – walked up, ready to go.

At the end of the day, the classroom a bustle of activity before the final bell, Bridget found Isaiah working in a corner, hunched over the art table, his face lined with concentration.

Isaiah had traced Bridget's angel pin on a piece of construction paper and had copied every detail, from the yellow halo to the light blue dress and the wide, wide wings. He eagerly handed the paper to Bridget, spilling out an explanation.

"You need a guardian angel, too," he said.

Bridget looked it over. The angel's eyes were off center, its halo was crooked and one wing was smaller than the other.

It was perfect.

"Why, thank you," Bridget said.

When the bell rang, sending the class scrambling for the door, Bridget found a small pair of scissors and carefully cut around the angel, then pinned it to the same spot on her coat.

Back on campus, Bridget Monroe set her backpack down to sign in at Bradshaw Hall. The residence hall was the only one open over break, though only a few students had taken advantage of it.

"Hello," Bridget said brightly.

The clerk, without looking up from his magazine, gave a slight nod.

"Any mail?"

No reaction. She stared at him for a moment.

He very deliberately took out his earphones – Bridget could hear the loud, fuzzy tones – and slowly raised his eyebrows, awaiting a repeat of the question.

"Any mail?" Bridget asked, louder this time.

"Not yet," he said, putting the ear phones back in.

This would become part of Bridget's routine for the next few days, as the calendar drew ever closer to Christmas. She'd do a morning shift at the mall, come back to the residence hall, check for mail, then head up to her room to open the few cards that had arrived. She could picture the rest filling up the mailbox back home. In the evening, Bridget would watch Christmas specials or old movies in the TV lounge, usually with a bag of microwave popcorn on the couch next to her.

It wasn't supposed to be like this, of course. That fall, she had quickly bonded with a group of women on her floor. And they had promised to watch out for her, to somehow make Christmas right.

But then Maria was surprised with a last minute plane ticket home to Puerto Rico. And Michelle, who had invited Bridget home with her, had to fly to Florida because her grandmother fell ill. That left Jen, who lived a few hours away, coming to pick her up.

If would be a taste of family, even if it wasn't her own.

So on Christmas Eve, as Bridget worked her shift at the mall, desperate for a familiar face, she counted the hours until Jen would arrive. She was so lost in the idea that when she returned to Bradshaw Hall, she didn't even stop at the front desk.

"You have a message."

Surprised, Bridget turned.

"A message?"

The clerk dug through a small pile of papers on the desk, finally handing a pink slip to her. It had Jen's name and number on it, the word "Urgent" under-lined.

Bridget pulled out her phone to call and realized she had missed a message there as well. She listened to it as she walked to her room, growing sadder with each step. It was Jen. The snow storm had started earlier than expected up north. And it was heavy. The highways were closed.

And Jen wasn't coming.

Bridget stepped into her room, plugged in the lights on her tabletop Christmas tree and noticed the message light on the desk phone was flashing. There was no need to check it. She knew the bad news that was behind the blink.

With a shiver from the cold, Bridget Monroe stepped into church and slowly climbed the stairs. The old church an-chored the campus, its steeples framing the sky, its bells marking the start of each class session. Bridget had decided to go to Midnight Mass and searched the arriving crowd – smiles everywhere but not a single familiar face.

With that, her heart sank ever deeper.

Bridget sat off to the side, continually checking her watch, as if to signal to others she was expecting someone to arrive. But as the church filled, she gave up the spot, just as the music for the procession began. As the priest made his way down the center aisle, Bridget spotted Jessie, the friendly custodian from Bradshaw Hall, across the way.

Jessie offered a warm smile and a small wave.

Bridget tried to smile back, but couldn't. Immediately, she felt bad. After all, Jessie always had a kind word for the freshmen in the hall. She took to them as if they were her own grandchildren.

During Mass, as the familiar carols filled the church, the rituals of the ceremony should have provided comfort. But Bridget found herself thinking of the cathedral back home, where the smoke of the incense would be carried to the ceiling along with the deep notes of the organ. How her family, with all the cousins, would fill an entire pew.

She shook her head, but couldn't shake the lonely thoughts.

When the Mass was over, Bridget stepped outside into a changed world.

There was snow everywhere.

Not a lot, but just enough to cast a white glow on the sidewalks, the trees, the buses, the cars, everything. The snow glittered in the streetlights, as if tiny diamonds had been mixed in with the light powder. As Bridget turned, taking it all in, two boys raced past, then skidded into long, laughing slides.

Bridget stood for a moment in the shadow of the church – its stained glass windows glowing against the dark sky –

and felt for the first time everything would
be just fine. She caught a few flakes on
her bare hands, then walked back to
Bradshaw Hall, humming carols along
the way.

As she walked, she found herself
thinking about Isaiah and his snow angel
demonstration. So, outside the building
she plopped to the ground to try one herself. As she looked at the swirl of snowflakes dancing through the night sky, she
closed her eyes and made a wish, but
dismissed it as quickly as she stood up.

Nobody actually gets a guardian angel,
she thought

Bridget was still humming when she
got off the elevator and saw the most surprising thing – a small box with a green
bow and shiny red paper sitting on the
floor outside her door. Her name was on
the package, but there was no sign of who
it was from. She picked up the box,

turned it over in her hands, searching for an answer.

Inside her room, she tore off the paper, opened the box and pulled out a pair of hand-made wool mittens, flecks of gold mixed in with the navy blue.

She looked them over, amazed at how perfect it all was.

Then she sat at the window, mittens on, and watched the snow drift to the ground, thinking of home, which no longer seemed so far away.

The next morning, Bridget asked at the desk about who had left the package, but the clerk said no one had come in. And none of the other students seemed to know anything about it. She called her friends, thrilled to hear their voices, but no one owned up to the surprise.

Neither did her parents, when they called before lunch.

Bridget decided to take a quick walk around campus, snapping photos of the snow so she could send them to her friends back home. When she finally returned to her room, she found another package outside the door.

This time, it was a matching hat.

For days, this went on.

One day, it was a mug and a packet of hot chocolate mix. Another day it was peppermint sticks. Another a book to read, still another a scarf – everything a girl from California could use to fight off the Midwestern cold.

When Bridget finally flew home, everything was just as she had pictured it, all the decorations, all the details. Her family pretended it was Christmas morning, but it was hardly the same. There was no magic to these gifts, no magic at all. And no surprises.

They were just all the things from her list.

In late January, on the morning of the first day of class, Bridget stood outside Bradshaw Hall talking with her friends, the group able to close a five-week gap in five minutes. All of them – Maria, Michelle and Jen – assured Bridget they had nothing to do with the mystery gifts.

"You know what?" Maria said. "You've got a guardian angel."

"Or a secret admirer," said Michelle.

Speculation quickly centered on the guy who always saved Bridget a seat in history class, a lecture hall that seated several hundred. As they talked, a cheery voice came from behind them.

"Welcome back."

It was Jessie, the longtime custodian, arriving for work. As usual, she had a smile on her face and gathered each of the girls into a hug.

"I sure missed seeing you girls over break," Jessie said, then added: "Although I did see one of you."

With that, she winked at Bridget, who quickly remembered ignoring her at Midnight Mass.

"Oh, I'm so sorry I didn't wait for you," Bridget said. "I just –"

But Jessie shook her head.

"Now," she said, "you know that's not what I'm talking about."

As she spoke, she took Bridget's hands in her own, and Bridget realized Jessie was wearing a pair of mittens – handmade, blue yarn with flecks of gold. Just like the ones Bridget had found outside her door on Christmas Eve.

"Well," Jessie said, looking at her watch. "Got to get to work, you know."

As the other girls headed to class, Bridget went back inside, catching up with Jessie in the lobby.

"How can I ever thank you?" Bridget asked.

"No," Jessie said. "How can I ever thank *you*?"

"But I didn't do anything," Bridget said. "You were the one who –"

Jessie raised her hand, gently cutting her off. Bridget waited as Jessie pulled out her wallet and slowly opened it, revealing a picture of little Isaiah, his eyes bright and his smile wide.

"My grandson," Jessie said simply.

And like that, it all fell into place.

"So, you're my guardian angel," Bridget said.

"No," Jessie replied. "You're mine."

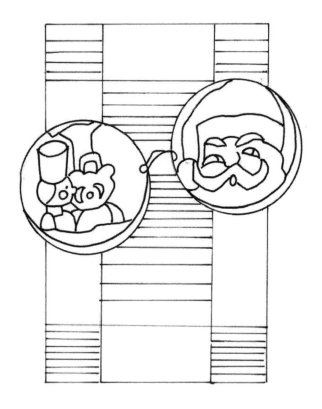

The Boy Who Saved Christmas

Ducking his head to avoid being noticed, Santa Claus stepped onto the sidewalk and into the massive rush of people. With a tall, twisted walking stick and an old brown fedora, Santa should have stood out in the downtown office crowd, but everyone swept past, faces grim and shoulders slumped, no one happy at all.

On that count, Santa himself fit right in.

He had barely gotten his bearings
when a man, briefcase in one hand and a
cell phone pressed to his ear, banged into
him, nearly knocking him to the ground.
The man glared at him and instantly sized
up his long beard and round belly.

"C'mon, Santa man," he sneered.
"Watch where you're going."

With scarcely a glance over his shoulder, the man disappeared into the crowd.
And for a moment, Santa was worried –
to think, Santa Claus himself discovered
wandering this far from the North Pole
mere days before Christmas! But the in-
cident barely registered a blip for the others, all hustling along in the shadows of
the afternoon.

Santa stopped at the entryway of Merton's Department Store and, before going
inside, paused to take in the holiday
scene. Bright flags lined the sidewalk,
snapping in the wind. Tiny lights filled
the bare trees and circled the store win-

dows, which featured elaborate scenes of mechanical reindeer and dancing elves. A scout troop was pressed up to the glass, the boys jostling to see the wonders inside.

Their excitement gave Santa Claus a new sense of hope.

So holding his walking stick for support, Santa closed his eyes, took a deep breath, waited a long moment and then quickly opened them.

But nothing had changed.

The world remained gray.

There was no blue in the scouts' uniforms, no red in the banners over the store's entryway, no yellow in the school bus that waited at the curb. To everyone else the scene appeared perfectly normal. But to Santa, it was as if he had stepped into an old movie scene, where every glorious color was reduced to gray.

Santa slowly shook his head.

"And I thought this was the place," he said quietly.

To be sure, Santa Claus didn't just *want* this to be the place. He *needed* it to be the place if this Christmas was going to be, well, Christmas at all. It was all related to an essential, but often misunderstood, part of the magic of the holiday, the magic that allows reindeer to fly and Santa himself to crisscross the globe in a single night, gifts in hand.

That magic, you see, is not eternal.

It does not live in the heart of Santa, but in the hearts of children, along with innocence and hope and love itself. Without all of that, the world is drained of joy and happiness. For Santa Claus, it is – quite literally – drained of color.

But once a year the magic can be renewed.

It requires no more than for Santa to look into the heart of a child and see not wishes for new toys or new things, but to see something pure and true. So every year, as the wind blows colder, Santa Claus sets out into the world, always in disguise, on a quest to preserve Christmas. For centuries, this worked without fail.

This year, though, was more desperate than most.

And that is what brought Santa to Merton's Department Store on this day, the 23rd of December.

Since the start of the month, he had made dozens of such stops at stores and malls and schools, at each secretly replacing one of his "helpers" so he could listen to the children himself, hoping for that one pure wish. But it never came. And with each passing day, Santa's world became more and more gray, the prospect of Christmas more and more remote.

Now, Santa pulled his coat tighter against the wind and, with a nod to the tired bell-ringer at the doorway, went inside.

He had to save Christmas.

But he couldn't do it alone.

Usually, when Santa Claus entered a store, even in disguise, children would begin to point and follow him, smiles on their faces. This time, unnoticed in his drab outfit, Santa slipped into the crowd and followed the signs to "Christmastown," the copyrighted version of the North Pole that was new this year at Merton's.

The display featured ice-skating penguins, each with a dapper red bow tie, and dancing polar bears, complete with green stocking caps.

Santa shook his head. In all his years, he had never seen any of that back home.

As he took the escalator to the second floor, he looked over the store below: shoppers everywhere, balancing bags in their arms as they reached for wallets and purses to pay for the next round of gifts; clerks carrying boxes to restock the shelves; kids tugging at the arms of their parents, eager to add to their wish list.

Now that, that he had seen at every stop.

At the top of the escalator, there was a commotion – a crowd of people and a chatter of noise that all but drowned out the cheery carols piped in as background music. Santa discovered it was a line, one that doubled back on itself so many times it was more like a tangle of bodies. Everyone, it seemed, was impatient, arms crossed, toes tapping.

"Excuse me," Santa said politely. "Is this ..."

"Yeah, the line for Santa," came the response. "Only the end is back there."

The man pointed, and Santa could see that the line started in the men's department, then wound through house wares, hardware and then – finally – "Christmastown" and its racks and racks and racks of toys.

"No skips."

The terse words came from a boy with a determined face. The boy's father pulled him close, as Santa turned, surprised at the tone.

"Well, I wouldn't dream of it," Santa said, trying to hide his heavy heart with a cheery voice. "I have other plans anyway. If you'll excuse me."

With that, Santa Claus smiled and headed down a nearby aisle.

No one else in line had noticed the man with the full gray beard and the twisted walking stick and the ample belly. No one, that is, except a small boy toward the back, one of the scouts from the troop that was outside. The boy, no more than 6, stepped out of line and eyed the man suspiciously, following the top of the walking stick through the racks of clothes as Santa made his way toward the back wall.

Like everyone else in line, Charlie Decker was impatient.

He had waited for this day for weeks, the day his scout troop would make its annual visit to see Santa. For Charlie, the visit was a special treat. He and his mother had moved in with his grandparents a few months back. But his mother was working extra hours, his grandmother didn't drive and his grandfather kept putting off the Santa visit.

To Charlie, his grandfather seemed to be sad lately.

Oh, he tried to disguise it when trading knock-knock jokes over dinner or accepting a good-night kiss. But these days he was always too tired to play games or read bedtime stories, let alone finish the model car they had started.

And he was acting funny, almost distant.

One day, when Charlie's class went to the city library, Charlie spotted his grandfather and waved, but his grandfather didn't wave back. When he asked about it that night at dinner, his grandfather said he wasn't at the library at all – he was at work, of course.

As the scouts talked and laughed, some trading baseball cards, others scanning the toy shelves, Charlie tugged on the sleeve of a chaperone.

"How much longer?"

Having slipped through a door marked "Employees only," Santa Claus found himself in a long hallway. Through the air vents, he could hear the hum of the conversation in the line outside. If he listened closely, he could distinguish some of the voices – there was Michelle and

Joe, Colleen and Marie, Carlos, Zavier and Rose.

Outside a plain door marked "Dressing Room," Santa paused to look at the posted schedule – "Broyles, 2 p.m. to 6 p.m." – and, with the slightest of nods, the door locked shut with a sharp click.

As he continued down the hall, Santa underwent a gradual transformation. His boots became a polished black, his faded jacket the familiar red overcoat, his beard the whitest of whites. By the time he reached the end of the hallway, he no longer held a twisted wooden rod, but a golden staff topped with an ornate snowflake.

Sleigh bells jangling, Santa stepped into the store with a hearty "Ho, ho, ho."

A cheer went up from the kids near the front of the line, and as word was passed down the line – "He's here!" "Santa's here!" – the buzz of excitement grew.

"You're late."

The words carried a snap to them.

Santa turned to see a tall woman in a blue dress, her hair pulled back in a tight ponytail. She held a clipboard against her chest and had a stressed look on her face. Her name tag identified her as Meredith.

Santa reached out to shake her hand and said hello. She was momentarily confused, but the gesture softened her tone.

"That's OK," she said. "We can still get through a lot of them if we try."

She checked her watch, then the clipboard.

"Now, remember we're pushing Rocky the Robot toys. They're on special."

Santa was dismayed.

"Is that what this is about?" he asked. "Selling?"

She looked at him, bewildered, as if she had to explain the most obvious thing to a small child.

"Well, there is a commission, you know," she said.

"Yes, of course," Santa said, absently.

She fluffed his beard, adjusted his collar.

"There," she said. "Now you look just like Santa."

"But, I am – " he said, before catching himself. "Never mind."

For the next few hours, the line inching ever forward, Santa sat patiently in his chair, welcoming child after child to his lap, always offering a smile, a hug, a gentle pat on the back. And the children came, spilling out their wishes, lists and lists of wishes – a race car, a fire truck, a puppy, a doll house with windows that open. One wanted a rocket launcher, another a pirate ship. It was a blur of "I want, I want, I want."

Santa thought back to the days when the wishes were simpler, for small things. In those days, any gift would do, it didn't have to be "new and improved" or "turbo charged." In those days, the world never dimmed to gray.

As the voices around him became a mumble and the scene began to grow fuzzy, Santa was startled by a yank on his beard.

"Santa, Santa, did you hear me?" asked the boy on his lap.

Santa looked down.

"Well, but of course."

"It's OK," the boy said in a matter-of-fact tone. "I know you're not real. I already gave a list to my mom and dad. They always get me what I want."

As the boy climbed down and walked away, Santa felt the day grow even gloomier.

There was a short delay, and then a bit of a bustle.

At the front of the line was a boy wearing his blue scout uniform, a dash of blond hair peaking out from under the hat, which itself was slightly askew. The boy had a face full of freckles, a pair of wire-rim glasses and wore a serious expression, though Santa knew there'd be dimples if only he would smile. He stopped in front of Santa, but before he climbed aboard Santa's lap, he stuck out a small hand.

"Hi," he said. "I'm Charlie Decker."

"Well, hello Charlie," Santa replied, amused by the formality. He shook the boy's hand in an exaggerated fashion. "I'm Santa ... Santa Claus."

"Oh," said the boy, his face suddenly sad.

"What's the matter, young man?" said Santa.

"Well, if you were real," the boy said, "your name would be Kris – Kris Kringle. I heard about it during story time at school."

"Well, funny that you say that," Santa said. "That is but one of my names. Some call me Father Christmas, some call me

Nicholas. But most just say Santa. Whatever you prefer."

The boy climbed into his lap.

"Now, what is your Christmas wish?"

"I don't want anything," the boy said
simply.

"Surely there's something."

Charlie shook his head. Despite more
prodding from Santa–maybe a basketball?
– Charlie was steadfast. No. Nothing at
all. He would like a basketball, sure. Anyone would. But Charlie, it seemed, had
something more serious on his mind.

"All I want," Charlie said finally, "is to
see my grandpa happy again."

Santa Claus was taken aback.

He looked deep into Charlie's eyes and
when he did, he saw the image of an
older man, shoulders slumped, sitting in
a small room and wearing a red and white
Santa suit. He instantly knew it was the
man he had left locked in the back room
and he instantly knew the whole story,

the shame of the man's lost job at the bank, the pain of making ends meet this way, the weight of hiding it all from his family, from Charlie. He looked deeper and could see the man's next day, and the next after that, each one a little bit brighter than the last.

The boy had a tear forming in his eye.

"Is that your true wish?" Santa asked.

"Yes," Charlie said, nodding eagerly.

Santa gently wiped the tear from his cheek.

Charlie's eyes were the bluest of blues, a bright, sparkling blue. Santa saw himself reflected in the boy's glasses, his outfit a deep, bright red – and when he looked up, he realized there was color everywhere, in the blinking lights on the trees that surrounded them and on the wreathes that hung above. There was color in the children and the walls and the carpets and – just like that – magic was again in the air.

He wanted to shout, to jump up and dance, but instead marveled at the boy on his lap, the boy who had no idea he had just saved Christmas

"That wish," Santa Claus said, his heart warm and light. "That wish will come true."

And he pulled Charlie into a deep hug.

After the shift was over, Meredith set about tidying up the area and Santa Claus wandered back into the hallway. When he reached the dressing room, he leaned his golden staff against the wall and – without opening the door – slipped inside.

The man he had seen in the boy's eyes was leaning over the sink, adjusting a long white beard in the mirror. His face was tired, his back stooped. The man fussed with his appearance for a moment, then stopped and rubbed a spot free in the mirror and – in the reflection – his eyes fixed on Santa. The man nodded and Santa offered a wink.

"Don't worry, they didn't miss you out there," Santa said in a voice that was at once reassuring and a bit jolly. "And, if you're looking for a gift for Charlie, I'd recommend a new basketball this year."

"Charlie?" the man said, turning so fast he nearly lost his balance. "How do you know ..."

But Santa had already disappeared.

In the hallway, his appearance returned to the drab look of before. He took his walking stick in hand and gave a quick nod toward a bulletin board, where a job notice magically appeared: Merton's Department Store, credit department.

Then he walked down the hallway, footsteps light, quietly whistling a Christmas melody.

Acknowledgments

When promoting *The Christmas Heart*, I often found myself scheduled for readings at libraries. This was the perfect setting, I thought, because from the beginning these stories were meant to be shared.

The stories are a product of a Christmas tradition of mine, in which each year I write a new story and send it to family and friends with my Christmas cards. For many, the stories have become a tradition as well, whether read together as a family on Christmas Eve or copied and shared with others, who pass them on again. The stories have also developed a devoted following among readers of the *Milwaukee Journal Sentinel*, where I work as a reporter.

For me, a highlight of Christmas is the moment when I drop a stack of Christmas cards in the mail, knowing the stories are about to be shared.

While writing can be a solitary endeavor, publishing a book is not.

Thanks to Badger Books and William Dries, for turning a Christmas book into a Christmas series. Jan Walczak, a longtime friend of the family, again contributed the beautiful illustrations.

My wife, Katy, is an amazing source of love and support ... and has a knack for spotting the holes in my stories. The same goes for my sister, Amy Ryan, and mother, Mary Anne Borowski-Lutz, who are always among the first to read them. Thanks, too, to the rest of my family, from brothers David and Mark, to their wives, Jodie and Kris, to the husbands of my mother and sister, George Lutz and Steve Ryan.

And, of course, the entire Flierl family, which has treated me as one of their own from the time I met Katy. Jenn Flierl was a particular help in pulling together the layout details for the cover.

Others who deserve thanks include Jim Higgins at the *Journal Sentinel*, who always leaves the stories better than when they arrived. Friends and co-workers Tom Kertscher and Ron Smith provided a valuable, final set of eyes on the stories.

Finally, thanks to everyone who bought the first Christmas book – but especially to those who passed it on to others.

– *Greg Borowski*

Also by Greg Borowski

The Christmas Heart
Best fiction, 2005 Midwest Book Awards

"A holiday treasure...captures the magic of the season."
--*Green Bay Press Gazette*

"Six heartwarming stories exude a Midwestern feel."
--*Oshkosh Northwestern*

"Reveals the magic of Christmas."
--*Milwaukee Journal Sentinel*

Also by Greg Borowski

First and Long
Best sports, 2004 Midwest Book Awards

"Immensely readable...this engagingly written account infuses personality into the players, staff and students... Those who love high school football will find themselves rooting for this diverse group of kids who never gave up."
--Booklist review

"Borowski seems to find all of America in a one-mile stretch of Capitol Drive in Milwaukee. *First and Long* is a compelling account of rich and poor, black and white. Urban and suburban youth all trying – against long odds - to move to the same snap count."
---Steve Rushin, *Sports Illustrated* columnist